HOW TO

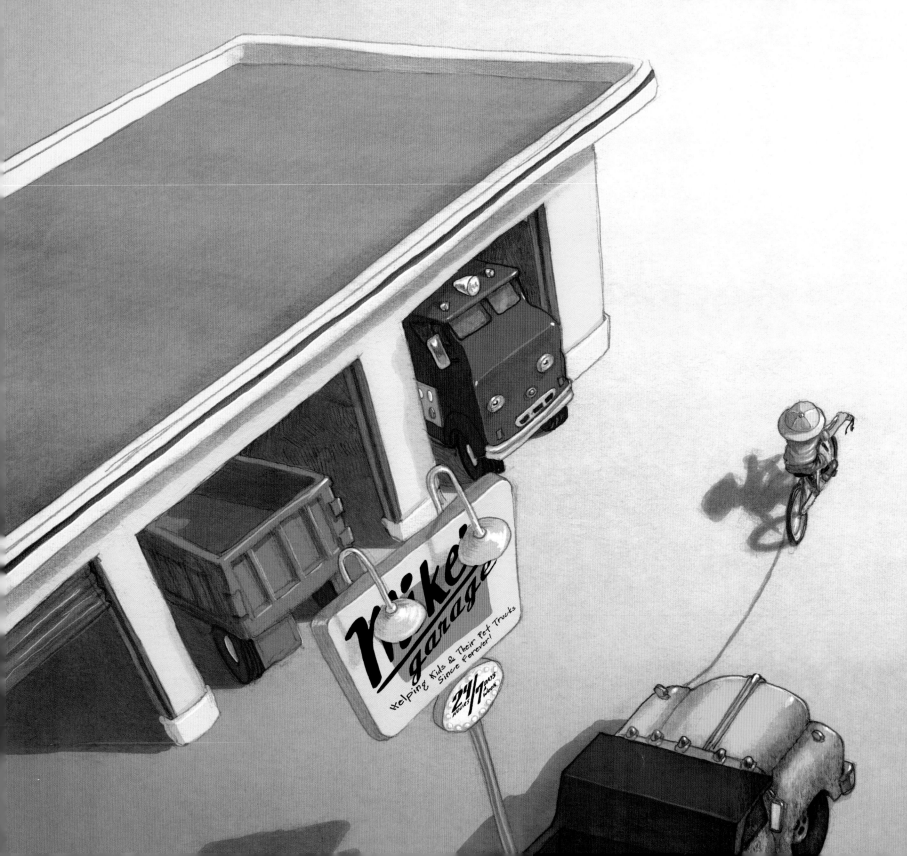

TRACK A TRUCK

JASON CARTER EATON

illustrated by **JOHN ROCCO**

CANDLEWICK PRESS

If you want a pet truck—and who doesn't?—
you've come to the right person! I've got two dump trucks and
a fire engine myself. I think everyone should have one!
And that's why I wrote this book. By the time you're done,
you'll know everything you need in order to track,
catch, and tame your very own pet truck.

Obviously, you can't just walk down to your local pet store
and say, "May I please have a tow truck?"
They'd think you were bananas! Trust me; I've tried it.
No, you have to look for your truck in its native habitat.

PETS

More interested in a monster truck?
They like to lurk in abandoned parking lots.

Garbage trucks can be found pretty much everywhere.

Pick a breed that's right for your home.
If you live in a small apartment,
a car transporter may not be a wise choice.

And remember, every fall, ice-cream trucks migrate south . . .

while snowplows head farther north.

Have you decided what kind of truck you want?
All right. Then it's time to track one down.

Look for signs and clues. You'll have to do some sleuthing.

And always keep an eye out for truck tracks.

Follow the tracks until you find your truck.

Now the fun part: catching it.

Wait until the truck notices you,
and then lay down a trail of orange cones.
Trucks can't help following orange cones.

Gee, I wish I had some way to move all this dirt.

Lead your truck to a useful project.
Trucks like to feel useful.
It will probably get straight to work.

Now comes the most important part:
give the Universal Truck Signal!
(Just make a fist and pull it down twice.)
Honk! Honk!

Great job!

If your truck responds . . .

you're good to go!

What will you name your truck?

Amelia

Quinn

Dusty

BarP

Mega-Marzipan

Professor Porkpie

Señor Waterloo

Introduce your pet truck to its new home.
Be sure it has plenty of room to play and explore.

Better yet, take it out to play with other trucks.
While it may take them some time to get the hang of playing together . . .

once they do, it's pure magic!

And that's all there is to it.

Congratulations!

You now know everything there is to know
about having a pet truck.

Treat your truck with kindness and love,
and you'll both be . . .

GOOD TO GO!

For my dad, the guy who inspired
my love of vehicles . . . with a parking ticket!
J. C. E.

To Mike Rejto, his 1972 F250,
and the adventures we had
J. R.